The Terrible Birthday Present

ANGELA BULL

Illustrated by Jacqui Thomas

Oxford University Press

Oxford University Press, Great Clarendon Street, Oxford OX2 6DP

Oxford   New York
Athens   Auckland   Bangkok   Bogota   Bombay
Buenos Aires   Calcutta   Cape Town   Dar es Salaam
Delhi   Florence   Hong Kong   Istanbul   Karachi
Kuala Lumpur   Madras   Madrid   Melbourne
Mexico City   Nairobi   Paris   Singapore
Taipei   Tokyo   Toronto   Warsaw

and associated companies in
Berlin   Ibadan

Oxford is a trade mark of Oxford University Press

© Angela Bull 1998
First published 1998

ISBN 0 19 918576 X   School edition
ISBN 0 19 918593 X   Bookshop edition

Printed in Great Britain by Ebenezer Baylis

Illustrations by Jacqui Thomas c/o Linda Rogers Associates

Photograph of Angela Bull by courtesy of the Craven Herald

Chapter 1

The birthday present was a big mistake!

Holly had gone to help in Aunty Sue's craft shop, one Saturday. That morning, they were putting some blue and pink cushions in the window.

Just then, two girls walked past, outside.

One girl wore a plain black skirt.

One girl wore a very bright, tartan skirt.

'Isn't that lovely!' cried Holly, looking at the black skirt.

'Yes, gorgeous!' agreed Aunty Sue, looking at the tartan skirt.

I'd love a skirt like that...

'Would you?' said Aunty Sue. She remembered that it was Holly's birthday next week.

Holly had a lot of presents on her birthday. Mum and Dad gave her a jacket.

Her sister Lucy gave her a hairclip.

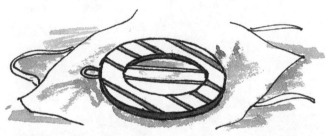

Her little brother Robin gave her a packet of fudge.

She had money from Gran, and a pile of cards.

'Hasn't Aunty Sue sent anything?' asked Lucy.

At that moment, the doorbell rang.
There was Aunty Sue. She was carrying
a big parcel.

'I've bought you a special present,
Holly,' she said. 'I know you'll
like it.'

Holly untied the
ribbon and pulled back
the paper.

A swirl of colours, red and yellow,
gold and orange, blazed out at her.
Holly stared.

It was a tartan skirt.

Holly had never seen anything so
bright. The reds and golds, yellows and
oranges, whizzed up and down in
stripes and checks. Just looking at
them made Holly feel sick. Sick and
dizzy.

'It's a proper kilt, all the way from Scotland,' Aunty Sue explained. 'You liked that tartan skirt outside my shop window. So I decided to buy one for you.'

'Wow!' gasped Robin.

It's like a million football strips mixed up together!

Lucy was holding on to Scooby-Doo,
her puppy. Scooby-Doo had sharp little
teeth. He loved biting sheets of paper.
Lucy was so busy trying to stop him,
she didn't notice the skirt.

'It's a lovely present,' said
Mum and Dad. Then everyone
looked at Holly.

Holly swallowed. It wasn't the tartan skirt she'd wanted. It was the black one. The skirt Aunty Sue had bought her was the ugliest skirt she'd ever seen.

She opened her mouth to say so, and shut it again.

All the family were smiling, thinking she was pleased.

'Oh,' she gulped. 'It's –'

She stopped. She didn't know what to say!

'Try it on,' urged Mum.

I'll take it up to my room.

She ran away, as fast as she could, with the terrible present.

In her bedroom, she took off her jeans. She fastened the kilt round her waist.

Stripes of red, yellow and orange blazed at her from the mirror. She felt lumpy and ugly.

I hate it, thought Holly. It's awful! I wanted a black skirt.

But she didn't know how to say so.

She made herself run downstairs. She gave Aunty Sue a kiss.

'Thank you,' she mumbled. 'It's lovely.'

Nobody guessed she was telling a lie.

Chapter 2

The tartan skirt was horrible. But Holly liked Aunty Sue a lot. She couldn't tell her she hated it. And she did hate it.

Sometimes she looked at it, hanging in the cupboard. It was like all the fireworks from Bonfire Night, and all the fruit from the supermarket, squashed into one horrible, dizzy pattern. Awful!

At last she decided to ask Lucy about it. Lucy was younger than her, but she knew a lot more about clothes. She always knew what looked good.

Lucy had had a peep at it in the cupboard, when Holly wasn't there. She thought the tartan skirt was terrible! But Holly had told Aunty Sue it was lovely. Maybe she really liked it.

'It's OK,' said Lucy, not looking at
Holly.

Holly sighed.
Now she couldn't
even tell Lucy about
the skirt. Lucy said
the skirt was OK.
Maybe it was.

'Aunty Sue's asked
you to help in the shop,'
Mum told Holly next Saturday.
'She'd be really pleased if you wore
your tartan skirt.

'Robin's going to paint his bedroom
chair, with that white
paint Dad didn't
need, so he'll be
busy –'

'And I'm going to teach Scooby-Doo to catch a ball,' said Lucy.

Holly went slowly upstairs, and took off her jeans. She looked hard at her tartan skirt in the mirror.
It was even worse than she remembered.

She pulled her longest sweatshirt down over it, as far as she could.

'Pleased with the skirt?' asked Aunty Sue cheerfully, when Holly arrived.

17

Holly helped in the shop all morning. It was quite fun. But when people came in, she hid behind the counter. She didn't want them staring at her tartan skirt.

Mum fetched her home for dinner.

'You must see Robin's chair,' she said. 'He's been painting it in the garage.'

'Hi!' called Robin, when he saw Holly. He was jumping up and down with excitement. 'Come and look at what I've done! I'm brilliant at painting. I'm better than Dad! I'm –'

He bounced against the stool where the paint can was standing.

It went flying. A great whoosh of white paint splashed out. All over Holly's tartan skirt!

Holly stared down at her skirt. Its bright colours were drowned under the enormous splodge of white.

Holly smiled and smiled.

Lucy and Mum rushed out to see what had happened.

'You careless boy, Robin,' Mum scolded. 'Look at poor Holly's new skirt! Never mind, Holly. I can soon clean it up for you.'

Holly's smile vanished.

It doesn't matter.

'Of course it does,' said Mum. She hadn't noticed Holly's face. 'Take it off. I'll see what I can do.'

Holly felt really fed up. For one marvellous moment she'd thought Robin had spoiled her skirt for ever. But no such luck! She crept sadly upstairs.

Lucy was thinking.

Why had Holly looked so pleased about her paint-splashed skirt? And why was she so miserable when Mum said she'd clean it?

It was very odd.

Chapter 3

Mum got the tartan skirt clean. And Holly couldn't forget it.

'Gran's coming round this afternoon,' said Mum next day. 'Why don't you put on your tartan skirt, Holly?'

Holly couldn't say no. Everyone thought she liked the tartan skirt. By now, it was too hard to explain that she didn't.

I've got to wear it, Holly told herself.

'My goodness!' said Gran, when she saw the tartan skirt.

What a bright skirt!

'Holly loves it,' said Mum.

Holly didn't speak. She knew she looked awful. She felt lumpy and awkward in those bright stripes and checks.

Suddenly her mood changed. She wouldn't go round looking terrible any longer, not even for Aunty Sue. She'd stop being good!

She picked up a cup of tea, and tipped it over.

A long dark stain ran all the way down her tartan skirt. Would that work? Holly held her breath.

'Oh, Holly!' cried Mum. 'How did you do that?'

'I just did,' said Holly. Her voice sounded loud and angry. But nobody seemed to notice.

'Never mind,' said Gran comfortably. 'Mum'll wash the tea out, and the skirt will be fine again.'

Fine! Holly scowled. She felt really angry!

'Take it off, and leave it on the washing machine,' said Mum.

The washing machine was in a corner of the kitchen. Robin's hamster lived in a cage, just nearby.

Holly looked at the skirt, and then she looked at the cage. She knew what hamsters could do.

She dropped her terrible tartan skirt beside the cage.

The hamster woke up. It saw something nice and chewy close to the bars. It didn't mind red and yellow checks. It stood on its back paws, and reached upwards.

Several mouthfuls of yummy tartan skirt were stored in its pouches. It was still munching when the family came into the kitchen.

Mum snatched the skirt away from the cage.

'Holly!' she exclaimed. 'You silly girl! Why did you leave your skirt next to the cage? Look at the holes the hamster's bitten.'

Holly didn't mind being called silly. When she looked at the holes, her eyes shone.

Please.

Maybe Robin's hamster had ruined her skirt for good.

But Mum was practical, as usual.
'I think I can mend it,' she said.
'They're only small holes.'
She carried the tartan skirt away.

Holly nearly cried.
She was never going
to get rid of her
terrible birthday
present!

Next Saturday morning, a brilliant idea hit her. She'd gone to the shop again, and Lucy had come too. Aunty Sue had been making toy trains. She'd used a big tube of superglue, and left it on a table.

Holly had put on her terrible tartan skirt. She looked at it, and then she looked at the superglue. Mum wouldn't get rid of that as easily as she'd got rid of paint and tea!

Quietly, she picked up the glue. She took off the top, and laid the tube on the floor.

It was just by the ladder Aunty Sue used for reaching things on high shelves.

Holly began to climb the ladder. She made up her mind that she'd slip – accidentally!

She'd crash off the ladder on to the tube. The superglue would squirt out all over her skirt –

And that would be that. You couldn't clean off superglue!

Holly took another step up the ladder. She wobbled it.

'What's that glue doing on the floor?' shrieked Aunty Sue.

She grabbed the tube, screwed on the top, and dropped it into a drawer. Holly stood on the ladder, frozen with dismay.

Lucy stared at her. She'd watched Holly putting the glue by the ladder.

Why had she done such a stupid thing? Now, looking at Holly's face, she remembered the paint, and the spilled tea, and the hamster holes. At last she understood.

Holly hated her tartan skirt!

Why didn't she say so? Lucy wondered. Perhaps she couldn't. Poor Holly! She just couldn't bear to upset Aunty Sue.

Lucy grinned. I'm not like Holly, she decided. I'd have said what I thought about that skirt. But now I'll have to find a way to help her!

Chapter 4

Mum got fish and chips for lunch.
Lucy was pleased. It would help her
plan nicely.

She waited till Holly was holding the
vinegar bottle. Then she joggled her
elbow. Vinegar splashed all over the
tartan skirt.

'I don't know what's wrong with you
girls,' scolded Mum. 'You do nothing
but spill things.'

'It's when Holly's wearing that skirt,' said Robin. 'The checks make people dizzy.'

'Rubbish!' said Mum. 'Though they are a bit dazzling. Take it off, Holly. I'll have to wash it again.'

Holly sighed. She didn't know that spilling vinegar was only the beginning of Lucy's plan.

Mum washed the skirt, and pegged it on the line. It flapped merrily in the wind.

Lucy peeped out. This was just what she'd hoped for. She went to find Scooby-Doo.

'Lovely games!' she told him. 'Biting games! Come on.'

Scooby-Doo ran after her, into the garden. He thought they were going to play. But Lucy stood on tiptoe, and pulled out a peg.

'There, Scooby-Doo. Bite!' she whispered.

Scooby-Doo... BITE!

She ran back into the house. Holly was in her bedroom, feeling miserable. Suddenly she heard Lucy calling.

Mum! Holly! Everyone! Come quick!

39

Holly raced downstairs. Lucy was standing by the kitchen window.

'Look!' she shouted. 'Look at Scooby-Doo!'

The whole family gazed through the window, and gasped.

The terrible tartan skirt flapped nearly to the ground. It was low enough for Scooby-Doo's sharp little teeth.

Scooby-Doo was having a wonderful
biting game. A ribbon of tartan
streamed from his mouth.

Everyone rushed outside.

Stop!
Scooby
-Doo!

Lucy grabbed Scooby-Doo. Mum
pulled out the other peg, and Holly's
skirt fell to the ground. It was ragged
and torn, from top to bottom.

'That lovely skirt!' groaned Mum.
'Oh, bad dog!'

Is it?

'Is it – spoiled?' Holly asked.

'Yes. Look at it! What a shame,' said Mum.

'D'you know what I think?' said Robin. 'I think all those colours made Scooby-Doo go mad. Dizzy-crazy! Poor Scooby-Doo.'

'It is a very bright skirt,' said Mum. 'Too bright, really.'

'Mum!' cried Holly.

'I hated it,' said Holly.

'Hated it!' echoed Mum, very surprised. 'Why didn't you say?'

'I couldn't. I didn't want to tell Aunty Sue,' Holly explained.

43

Suddenly everyone looked at Lucy.

She was holding Scooby-Doo's collar.
'He's only a puppy. But, Mum,
Holly's going to need a new skirt.'

'Yes,' agreed Mum. 'Maybe we could all go and look this afternoon. You can have your pocket money early. And there's your birthday money, too.

'I saw some flowery skirts in the market you might like. They were pink and pale blue.
Very pretty.'

Holly took a deep breath. Her heart beat fast. This was her chance to speak out at last.

'Oh, Mum!' she said. 'What I'd like – what I really want – is a black skirt.'

'Black!' exclaimed Mum. 'I never thought of that. But it could be nice. It would certainly look better than tartan. Right. Let's go!'

In her mind, Holly saw herself walking into the shop. She was wearing a new black skirt. She looked cool and slim.

'I should have told Aunty Sue what I really liked,' she said. 'But it doesn't matter now. Scooby-Doo's made everything come right.'

About the author

Isn't it awful when you open a parcel, and find inside it just what you *don't* want! Do you tell people? Do you keep it quiet? That's Holly's problem when she opens her terrible  birthday present. She can't think what to do about it. She's really stuck. Long ago, I was rather like Holly. If I opened birthday books that looked boring, or clothes that were horrible, I didn't tell people. I just felt cross! Lucky Holly has Lucy and Scooby-Doo to help her.

I live in the country in Yorkshire, and I've written lots of children's books.

Also available in packs
| Stage 12 pack C | 0 19 918577 8 |
| Stage 12 class pack C | 0 19 918578 6 |